Gears in My World

Joanne Randolph

JOURNEYS®

Rosen Classroom
New York

For Linda Lou and Lucas

Published in 2007 by The Rosen Publishing Group, Inc.
29 East 21st Street, New York, NY 10010

First Edition

Photo Credits: Cover and p. 15 © Reuter Raymond/Corbis Sygma; Cover and pp. 5, 22 (gear) © Stockdisc/Getty Images; Cover and p. 19 © Annie Griffiths Belt/Corbis; pp. 7, 9, 11, 22 (axle, chain) © Royalty-Free/Corbis; p. 13 © PunchStock; pp. 17, 22 (engine) © Pitchal Frederic/Corbis Sygma; p. 21 © H. David Seawell/Corbis.

ISBN: 978-1-4042-8423-4
6-pack ISBN: 978-1-4042-9195-9

Manufactured in the United States of America

Contents

Gears are a kind of simple machine. People use simple machines to help them do work. A gear can be used to move things.

Gears look like wheels that have teeth. A gear is often made of at least two of these toothed wheels. The teeth allow the wheels to move each other.

A gear often has a part in the middle called an axle. This turns the wheel. The first gear can then move others that are touching it. Sometimes chains or belts move gears.

Picture two gears. One is bigger than the other. The larger gear will move more slowly than the small one. The large gear can do more work with fewer turns than the small gear.

Each gear turns in a different direction from the one before it. We have three gears. The first one turns toward the right. It moves the second gear toward the left. Which way will the third gear move?

A clock has gears in it. The gears allow the hands of the clock to move. The hands of the clock tell us the time.

A car has gears, too. The gears help the engine work. The engine makes the car run. The gears on this engine are connected by belts.

Bikes have gears. The gears let riders move uphill more easily. Without gears the riders would have to use much more force to pull the bike up the hill.

Can you think of gears you see around you? Look at this picture. Can you find the gears here?

Words to Know

axle

chain

engine

gear

Here are more books to read about gears:
Pulleys and Gears (Machines in Action)
by Angela Royston
Heinemann, 2003

Web Sites:

Due to the changing nature of Internet links, Journeys has developed an online list of Web sites related to the subject of this book. This site is updated regularly. Please use this link to access the list: www.powerkidslinks.com/mws/gears/

Index

Word Count: 257

Note to Librarians, Teachers, and Parents

Journeys books are specially designed to help emergent and beginning readers and English language learners build their skills in reading for information. Sentences are short and simple, employing a basic vocabulary of sight words, simple vocabulary, and basic concepts, as well as new words that describe objects or processes that relate to the topic. Large type, clean design, and stunning photographs corresponding directly to the text all help children to decipher meaning. Features such as a contents page, picture glossary, and index introduce children to the basic elements of a book, which they will encounter in their future reading experiences.